A novel based on the major motion picture

Adapted by James Ponti

Based on the screenplay
by The Wibberleys and Ted Elliott & Terry Rossio and Tim Firth

Based on a story by Hoyt Yeatman

Executive Producers
Mike Stenson, Chad Oman, Duncan Henderson, David James

Produced by Jerry Bruckheimer

Directed by Hoyt Yeatman

DISNEP PRESS

New York

Printed in the United States of America

First Edition
1 3 5 7 9 10 8 6 4 2

Library of Congress Catalog Card Number on file.
ISBN 978-1-4231-1287-7

For more Disney Press fun, visit www.disneybooks.com

SUBJECT: PROJECT CLUSTERSTORM

CLASSIFICATION: TOP SECRET

This file was compiled from various field reports, surveillance videos and agent debriefings. It represents the best available data with regard to the events surrounding Project Clusterstorm. It should be noted that while acknowledging a few of the test programs that examine the practicality of using animals to assist in intelligence gathering, the National Security Agency, the Federal Bureau of Investigation, and the Department of Homeland Security have never officially confirmed the existence of the group code-named G-Force.

Unofficially, however, the directors of these organizations would like to say that if you come across any animals—specifically guinea pigs—who appear to be in the midst of a surveillance operation, please do not interrupt or otherwise interfere with their mission. Furthermore, if they appear to be hungry, guinea pigs are known to enjoy a diet that includes diced carrots, lettuce, and apples. Your assistance in this matter will be greatly appreciated.

—Ben Kendall

Chapter 1

Night had fallen. In a bad part of town, a tall, bland-looking warehouse stood empty and dark—except for a single light moving along an upper floor.

Doctor Ben Kendall, a flashlight gripped tightly in his hand, moved cautiously down a warehouse hallway. In his other hand, he clutched a briefcase. Coming to a door, he glanced both ways. When he was satisfied the coast was clear, he opened the door and ducked inside. A table and two chairs were set up. A single lamp cast an eerie glow upon the room. Both chairs were empty.

With his scruffy beard and lumpy body, Ben looked more like a middle-school math teacher than a government agent. But, despite his appearance, Ben was the founder and leader of the G-Force. And he was about to send the agents on their first mission.

Taking a seat in one of the chairs, Ben nervously ran his fingers through his beard. He had absolutely no authority for what he was about to do, and that made him uneasy. But with the stakes so high he felt he had no choice. The future of the program—and perhaps the security of the country—were at stake.

"Thanks for coming," he said into the empty room. "The Feds are coming tomorrow to shut us down. There is only one way we can save this department."

Ben paused. He wanted to make sure that everyone understood the importance of what he was saying. He also wanted to make sure he had the courage to go through with it.

"And if we don't get our mission right, it could be our last," he added. He didn't say it out loud, but he mentally added, our *only* mission.

Agent Darwin was to take the lead. Like most federal agents, Darwin was a dedicated patriot determined to make the world safe. He was willing to put himself in harm's way to protect the people of the United States. But, in one very important way, Darwin was different from virtually every other federal agent.

Agent Darwin was . . . a guinea pig!

He wasn't the only one. The *G* in G-Force stood for *guinea pig*. In addition to Darwin, G-Force included Blaster and Juarez, who bickered like brother and sister yet could always count on each other to come to the rescue no matter what.

Blaster was a wise guy who loved to crack jokes no matter how tense the situation. He had enough attitude for an animal ten times his size.

Juarez, meanwhile, was a Latina beauty who had the looks and style of a supermodel—at least the guinea-pig version of a supermodel—but those who knew her weren't fooled by her long eyelashes. They knew she was one tough commando.

G-Force also included a mole named Speckles and a fly named Mooch. Despite being as blind as—well, a mole—Speckles was a computer mastermind capable of designing high-tech devices and surveillance systems as well as hacking into everything from national defense systems to highly secured mainframe computers.

Mooch was the eyes of the operation. He was trained to fly miniature nano-cameras into enemy territory ahead of the team in order to give them a complete layout of the surrounding area.

Ben had assembled a team that could revolutionize the world of spying and intelligence gathering. But first, he had to convince his bosses that the idea wasn't crazy.

The key to G-Force's success was its ability

to slip in and out of a hot zone without being seen. And now was their moment of truth. They *had* to complete their mission.

Having heard Ben's introduction, Darwin revealed himself. Taking a spot on his chair, he watched as Ben opened his briefcase. Inside was a hi-tech computer. Despite the low-tech surroundings, Ben's presentation looked like something out of a science-fiction movie. As he spoke, 3-D holograms appeared next to him as if they were floating in air. The first was a picture of a thin man with a devilish smile.

"Our target is Leonard Saber," Ben began. "He is a former arms dealer and current CEO of Saberling Industries, the world's largest manufacturer of household appliances."

Darwin eyed the picture carefully, burning the image of the enemy into his memory.

"The bureau's intel shows Saber has developed a new microchip with possible military applications," Ben continued. As he spoke, a hologram of a microchip floated next to him. "They think he might be selling this technology to the Far East under the code name Clusterstorm."

Waving his hand in the air, the chip disappeared. In its place was a schematic of Saber's mansion. Darwin waited for his orders.

"Your mission is to download the Clusterstorm files from Saber's personal computer, located in his study."

"Why haven't the Feds moved in?" Darwin asked.

"Feds can't touch him without evidence," Ben explained.

Darwin weighed this information. He knew his team could do it. But they needed to act—fast. "We move tonight," Darwin confirmed.

CHAPTER 2

With its massive stone walls, tightly sealed gates, and high-tech security systems, Leonard Saber's mansion was more like a fortress than a home. It was protected by a squadron of elite guards who patrolled and monitored the property night and day. They used state-of-the-art cameras, Doberman watchdogs, heat sensors, motion detectors and various classified technologies to protect Saber and his secrets from the outside world. In fact, many of these devices were designed and built by Saber's very own company, Saberling Industries.

But while the mansion's security was capable of withstanding a full-fledged assault by enemy agents, it was completely useless against the common housefly.

Not that there was anything *common* about Mooch. After all, not many houseflies have memorized the FBI handbooks for undercover surveillance, field reconnaissance, and pursuit evasiveness.

By the light of a full moon, he buzzed over one of Saber's massive walls, flew right up to the house, and gently landed on top of a Saberling 3000 security camera. He was looking for weaknesses in Saber's defense.

Finding them on this night would not be easy. Security was particularly intense because Saber was hosting a lavish party for industry leaders, financiers, and members of the media. A long line of expensive cars and limousines stretched down the street from the gated entrance, where guards checked invitations against a computer database that included facial-recognition software.

The guards were determined to make sure no uninvited guests crashed the party, but the G-Force was determined to do exactly that.

While Mooch was taking his position up high, Darwin was working from ground level. As he approached the estate he carefully avoided a pair of Dobermans patrolling the fence line. Darwin was always cautious around dogs. Unlike humans, dogs realized that other animals could be a threat. Still, he was confident that he could outsmart even the best-trained guard dogs.

"Who hires a security team that sniffs their own butts?" he scoffed as he watched them continue along the fence line completely unaware of his presence.

A voice called out over Darwin's earpiece. It was Speckles, who was running mission communications from a mole hole in front of the property. "Status report?" he asked.

Darwin dropped down low against the ground and slipped on a pair of night-vision goggles. He scanned the crowd until he locked on to Leonard Saber. Saber was wearing an expensive European suit and greeting guests at the main entrance to his home.

"I've got a visual on Saber," Darwin said into his mouthpiece.

Darwin adjusted the focus on his night goggles and carefully examined the billionaire. "He's wearing a six-thousand-dollar suit, a fifty-thousand-dollar watch, and according to my infrared scope, Hanes thirty-six-inch tighty whities."

Down in his hole, Speckles shook his head. Darwin and the other agents loved to crack jokes. They thought it made them look cool. Speckles, on the other hand, liked to keep things businesslike.

"Darwin, Saber is about to start his speech," Speckles reminded him. "Remember, the clock is ticking. Blaster, Juarez, what's your twenty?"

With Mooch in the air and Darwin on the ground, the last two members of the G-Force were underwater. Propelled by tiny underwater scooters, Blaster and Juarez had already navigated through a series of drainage pipes and waterways to reach a pond on Saber's property. Tiny headlights illuminated their way as they knifed through the murky water.

"Approaching first objective," Juarez responded into her intercom. A few moments later, she signaled Blaster, and they began to swim up toward the moonlight.

"Time to get this party started!" Blaster said as they broke the surface of the water and began to climb out onto the mucky shore. "Thanks for inviting us to your party, Mr. Saber. I just peed in your pond."

Juarez shook her head and laughed. She knew that Blaster just couldn't keep his mouth shut. Blaster smiled. He just knew that, even in the middle of a mission, Juarez couldn't help but look hot. He stared at her as she stepped out onto the shore, her wet fur glistening in the moonlight.

Juarez gave her body a rhythmic shake that practically moved in slow motion. As she did, water sprayed in every direction. In a flash, every hair had fallen perfectly back into place, and her coat was again flawlessly luxurious. His mouth fell open as he watched her.

"Blaster," she said, noticing that he was staring. "Don't drop a pellet."

Blaster gulped. "Too late."

From the water's edge, Blaster and Juarez rushed up to the mansion and fired grappling hooks onto the roof. It may have been their first official mission, but they were all moving with expert timing and precision.

Darwin, meanwhile, had quickly scanned the line of cars and noticed a sleek convertible being driven by a beautiful blond woman. He was confident he could slip into her car and then into the party.

"I'm going in with the blond," he informed Speckles.

"Now there's a shocker," Speckles said, oozing sarcasm.

Darwin reached the convertible driven by the beautiful blond in no time. The woman had a fur coat that was the same color he was. So he was able to slip into the coat's pocket and completely blend in. He rode in the pocket as she walked past security and into the main ballroom. Within moments, Darwin had jumped out of the coat and was scurrying across the expensive marble floor Saber had imported from Italy.

The next step in the plan was for the G-Force to raid Saber's study while he was giving his speech to the partygoers. It wouldn't give them much time. But it was the only way they could be sure he would be away from the study. They couldn't get started until Mooch had his eyes on Saber. The fly zipped and buzzed his way through the mansion with the nanocamera on his back. He needed to get in place, but Mooch couldn't help but be distracted by all of the mouth-watering desserts. After all, Mooch wasn't a *common* housefly, but he was still a housefly.

Speckles realized what was happening when he saw the desserts appear on the video screen down in his mole hole. "Mooch, focus," he called into the intercom. "You're not here for sweets. Get back on mission."

Mooch responded with a quick buzz and flew into the grand ballroom. It was elegant and very high-tech. Giant flat-screen televisions were set up around the room displaying images of Saberling's most popular products—everything from toasters and blenders to satellites and jet engines.

A beautiful young woman named Christa stepped up to the podium. She was Mr. Saber's personal assistant and was always nearby making sure things moved smoothly.

"May I introduce you to our host tonight,"

she announced to the large crowd. "CEO of Saberling Industries, Leonard Saber."

The crowd erupted into heavy applause as Saber took long, confident strides toward the podium. He was rich and successful. In this world he was a rock star, and the crowd hung on his every word.

"Welcome to my home. I know it's not much," he said with a wink, sending the party-goers into gales of laughter. "I want you to know how grateful I am to all of you for once again making us the number one consumer electronics brand in the world."

As Saber addressed the crowd in the ball-room, the G-Force began the second phase of their operation. They'd infiltrated the house, now they had to get into the study and hack into Saber's computer.

Blaster and Juarez got into position on the roof, while Darwin worked his way through the ventilation system into Saber's study.

"Okay, I'm in," Darwin said into his intercom

as he scurried into the room. "Clearing exfil route." *Exfil route* was spy lingo for escape path. Darwin's was supposed to be through the fireplace and up the chimney onto the roof. But there was a problem—a fire was burning in the fireplace.

Darwin scampered over to the fireplace and eyed it suspiciously. Speckles had given him specific directions, but they seemed hard to believe. Darwin clapped twice and the fire instantly went out. Saber had developed a sound-activated switch for the fireplace.

"It worked," Darwin said, sounding a bit surprised.

"Of course it worked," Speckles said. It frustrated him whenever the members of the G-Force doubted him. He was part of the team, but he felt like the others looked down on him.

"Nothing happens in this house that I don't know about," he bragged. "Trust me."

Darwin nodded and smiled. He trusted his

friend very much. Hurrying over to Saber's personal computer, he plugged a small portable hard drive into it. To hack into the system he had to work the keyboard, which wasn't easy for a guinea pig with his short legs.

He had to twist and turn and stretch his body into all different directions to touch the right keys on the keyboard. It seemed more like a Pilates lesson than typing, but after a few moments, a logo appeared on the computer screen. Written across the logo was the word CLUSTERSTORM.

Darwin flashed a big, guinea-pig smile and made an announcement over his communicator.

"I'm in."

Back in the grand ballroom, Saber was still addressing the partygoers.

"For years we've been putting a secret into the heart of every member of the Saberling family," he announced as he motioned to the video monitors, which displayed images of various Saberling products. "A secret that is at the core of any successful family—communication."

Just then, a logo appeared on the monitor behind him. It read SABERSENSE. Saber flashed a mysterious smile. The partygoers had no idea how big a development SaberSense truly was. In fact, they wouldn't know for a few days. And, by then, it would be too late.

Saber walked over to where a spotlight illuminated a Saberling coffeemaker.

"In forty-eight hours, this coffee machine will change the world. When I press this button," he said, pointing to the power switch, "it will activate a wireless system we call SaberSense, which will awaken the chips already in the logic boards of all Saberling appliances.

"On Friday," he went on, "SaberSense will link every old and new Saberling appliance in existence and create one big family—and nothing—nothing . . . will be the same."

Just then, a giant countdown clock appeared on the monitor behind him. It read 48:00:00, and it instantly began counting down to the moment that SaberSense would activate.

Although the audience in the ballroom didn't realize the ominous potential of this announcement, the audience down in the mole hole certainly did. Watching a live video feed from Mooch's nanocamera, Speckles did some quick figuring in his head.

There were millions of Saberling appliances and products across the world, and all of them were controlled by computer chips. If SaberSense technology allowed them to connect and communicate with each other, Leonard Saber had a link that reached inside virtually every home, office, and school. Considering Saber's background as an unscrupulous arms dealer, there was no telling how he might take advantage of this tremendous power.

Saber looked out at his audience, smug in the knowledge that they had no idea how much their world was about to change. "Thank you, and good night," he concluded.

CHAPTER 3

With Saber's speech completed, the G-Force went into high alert. He could come back to his study at any moment, and Darwin still hadn't finished hacking into his computer.

"Saber wrapped his speech," Speckles announced over the intercom. "Mooch, give me an eyeball."

Mooch left his spot at the back of the ballroom and buzzed over the audience until he was close enough to Saber to pick up personal conversations. He had to remain mobile because Saber was on the move, but he also had to make sure he didn't get too close. Swatting was a very real danger.

Saber walked over to his assistant, Christa, and leaned in so that none of the guests could hear. "I'm going upstairs for a drink," he informed her. "Get these people out by ten-thirty."

Watching on the video feed down in his mole hole, Speckles lit a fire under the others.

"Saber's heading up!" he announced. "ETA about fifty seconds!"

"Just enough time to check the score of the Lakers game," Darwin answered confidently, keeping his cool in the middle of an emergency. "Downloading to PDA now."

Darwin started to download the Cluster-storm file and noticed that the countdown clock on the monitor in the ballroom was now also on the computer screen.

Darwin figured that he could download the information in about forty seconds, which would give him ten to spare. But within moments, the image on the screen started to go crazy. Different pictures, diagrams, and bar codes began flashing in front of Darwin's eyes. It seemed as if the computer had taken on a life of its own.

"Whoa! What just happened?" Darwin called out.

"Encryption," Speckles announced as he monitored the situation from down in his mole hole. "Hands off the keys. I'm sending up a worm to decipher."

Speckles adjusted the thick eyeglasses he always wore and went to work. From his base in the mole hole he could instantly flash commands to the portable hard drive Darwin had plugged into the computer.

Darwin knew Speckles could break the code faster than anybody, but he also knew that he still might not have enough time.

"Mooch," he called out over the intercom. "You have to stop Saber."

In a flash, the housefly went from cameraman to field agent. First, Mooch tried to distract Saber by dive-bombing him. Saber took a couple of futile swats at the air but didn't come close to hitting him. On his next pass, Mooch went in for the kill by rocketing straight up and into Saber's nostril. He buzzed for a moment and sent Saber into some spasms.

While the fly was delaying Saber, Speckles's worm was deciphering the computer encryption. After a few moments of crazy images and bar codes flying by, the screen returned to normal.

"I'm back in! Commencing download!" Darwin informed the others. He dragged the icon for Clusterstorm over to his portable hard drive.

"Speckles, you're a genius!"

"I'm a mole," Speckles responded matter-of-factly. "I got a thing for worms." Just then, he spied an earthworm crawling across his mole hole. In one quick move he slurped it right up.

Mooch had done his best but finally had to retreat. Watching on the video feed, Darwin could see Saber just outside the door to the study.

"Switching to wireless download!" he whispered into the intercom. He typed in a command and unplugged the portable hard drive, which continued to download the program over its wireless feed.

Leaping off the table, Darwin quickly carried the drive over to his escape route in the fireplace. Unfortunately, the wireless setting slowed the download.

"Take your time," he said to the computer sarcastically. "No hurry."

On Mooch's video feed everyone could now see Saber entering the room.

Blaster and Juarez were at the top of the chimney, where they had set up a winch and a cable. They had dropped the cable down to the fireplace so they would be able to pull Darwin out the instant he was ready.

"Get out of there, now!" Juarez called out nervously.

Darwin looked down at the device. The download was still going. "I can't," he whispered. "The chimney will block the signal!"

Blaster and Juarez looked at each other and then looked down the chimney, feeling nervous and helpless.

"If he doesn't make it, are you free Thursday night?" Blaster asked, half-teasing. It was no secret he had a thing for Juarez. But her heart belonged to Darwin.

Juarez glared at him. "He'll make it," she said confidently.

Darwin looked up at the escape line hanging above his head and then down at the monitor. The download was almost complete, but he was running out of time.

Across the room, Saber entered and settled down into a chair with his drink. He was about to read some reports when he felt a chill in the air. He decided that a nice warm fire would be the perfect thing so he clapped twice to activate the fireplace.

It took a nanosecond for Darwin to figure out what was happening, but once he smelled the gas he knew the fireplace that he was hiding in was about to become a hot zone in every sense of the term.

"Now, Blaster!" he shouted as the fire started to spread. He jumped just ahead of the flames and grabbed on to the escape line. Up on the roof, Blaster threw the winch into high speed and Darwin zipped his way up the chimney inches ahead of the heat wave from the blaze below.

"Whoaaaa," Darwin called out as he shot out of the chimney like a cannonball. He landed on the roof with a loud thud.

Blaster and Juarez rushed over to him.

"Your butt's on fire," Blaster said frantically. "Stop, drop, and roll!" Blaster decided the only way to save his friend was to smother the fire with his body. He dived right at him.

Fire or no fire, Darwin didn't think he'd enjoy the feeling of Blaster's rather large body crushing him. He stepped out of the way, and Blaster flew right past him and slammed against the wall. Then Darwin coolly patted the flames out by himself. No fire, no Blaster bruises.

Darwin had stayed until the last possible moment. The big question was whether or not it was late enough. He took a deep breath and looked down at the monitor on the hard drive.

A flashing message told him everything he needed to know. DOWNLOAD COMPLETE.

"We got it!" Darwin happily announced into the intercom. "Speckles, exfil!"

"Way ahead of you," Speckles replied as he began to clear out.

While infiltrating a hot zone was hard, exfiltrating—or getting out—was even harder. A team could move slowly and carefully while sneaking into a location. But once a mission was complete, agents had to hurry because their cover could easily be blown.

"I'll be waiting at the entrance," Speckles said before he came to a grinding halt. Just inches in front of him he saw the muzzle of a Doberman digging down into the mole hole.

Very quietly, Speckles pushed his body back as far into the hole as it could go and called out for help. "Speckles reports a large canine at exfil." He started panting nervously. "No escape. Repeat, no escape!"

The rest of the G-Force instantly went into action and charged to the edge of the roof.

"Hang on, Speckles!" Darwin called out. "We leave no fur behind!"

Then, Darwin, Juarez, and Blaster, equipped with parachutes, all jumped off the roof.

As they began free-falling to the ground far below, they got into aerial formation. "Yippee!" shouted Juarez, enjoying the feel of the wind racing across her face.

"I'll take out the Doberman!" Blaster said as he rotated his body to point directly at the fierce dog.

After a few moments, they pulled their rip-cords and tiny parasails deployed. With expert navigating, they were able to zero in on the exact spot where the dog was terrorizing Speckles.

Blaster landed first—directly on top of the dog's head, catching him totally off guard.

Unfortunately, Blaster bounced off the dog . . . and straight into a bush. His parasail got caught on a branch, and Blaster was left dangling right out in the open. His pride quickly turned to fear when the Doberman moved away from Speckles and turned his snarling teeth toward him.

"Whoa! Nice doggie! Sit!" he cried with a sudden sense of panic. "Roll over! Play dead?"

The dog lunged forward to take a bite out of Blaster, but Juarez came to the rescue twirling a pair of *bolas* over her head. She expertly threw the rope that connected the heavy bolas right at the dog's mouth. The weights at the end of the rope quickly spun around until they had wrapped his muzzle completely shut, saving Blaster.

"We're out of here," Darwin said as he swooped into the mole hole to rescue Speckles.

While the dog was now safely snared by the bolas, his barking had attracted a lot of attention. A group of guards were rushing over to investigate.

The G-Force had to get out fast.

"By the way," Juarez said to Blaster as they sprinted toward safety, "I just saved your furry behind!"

Blaster nearly laughed. "That dog was about to roll over and fetch my slippers!"

Just then, the group turned the corner and stopped cold in their tracks. Right in front of them was any rodent's worst nightmare—an exterminator.

He wore a helmet and a gas mask and carried a canister marked with a skull and crossbones and the words, RODENT POISON, written across it. Looming over them, he was in perfect position to get the entire team.

Before they could react, the exterminator was pumping the canister and spraying a green gas right on top of them. In a matter of seconds, they were coughing and passing out one by one.

The guests watched in horror as the exterminator went about his business. He picked up the four bodies and loaded them into the back of his truck. In a matter of moments, the truck was rattling down the road away from Saber's mansion.

When they were a safe distance away, the exterminator pulled off his mask and helmet. It was Ben! He had provided the final twist to their brilliant escape plan.

"Okay, we're clear," he announced to them.

Juarez stopped pretending to be dead and sat upright, coughing. "That was a little heavy on the smoke, Ben!"

"Yo, Juarez, did you catch the little leg twitch at the end of my death?" Blaster asked as he sat up and smiled broadly. "That was acting, baby. I was feeling it!"

"Amazing. Tell me you're not part possum," Juarez shot back.

"You can laugh now," Blaster answered. "But some of those people were crying. It was like the end of *Old Yeller*."

Just then, Mooch flew in through the truck window and came to a perfect landing on Ben's forearm.

"Mooch, you made it!" Ben said gleefully. "How'd it go in there, guys?"

"The party's over for Saber," Darwin announced, holding up his portable hard drive. "It's all there. Clusterstorm, everything."

Ben let out a sigh of relief and gave a happy slap to the steering wheel. "I knew you could do this!"

First mission? Complete.

CHAPTER 4

The G-Force headquarters were located in a run-down warehouse that once housed Acme Extermination. To the outside world it still looked like a pest-control company. But Ben had converted the building into a lab for his experiments and a place for his G-Force team agents to train and live.

The morning after their daring mission into Saber's mansion, the G-Force team were doing their best to kick back and relax in their little apartments, which were stacked one on top of another.

Darwin was trying to meditate in his while he listened to classical piano music. But Juarez's funk music was playing so loudly, it shook the floor Darwin was sitting on. She had just gotten out of the shower and was blow-drying her hair when Darwin knocked on the door.

"Is the music too loud?" Juarez asked.

"No," said Darwin. "I appreciate the dynamic, highly syncopated polyrhythms."

Juarez stared at him. "I'll turn it down," she said, heading for her boom box. Darwin could be strange sometimes.

Ben was too nervous to pay attention to what was going on. His boss was due to arrive at any moment to review the G-Force program.

Ben was worried that he might get shut down so he wanted to make the best impression possible. He'd even put on a suit, although the only suit he owned was rumpled and snug across his belly.

Marcie Hollandsworth, the veterinarian for the team, had reassured him he looked sharp. Still . . .

Just then a buzzer sounded. Someone was at the front door.

"Okay, everybody," Ben called out. "They're here. It's showtime!"

The team turned off the music and got into their prearranged positions. They were all going to do their best to help Ben make a good impression.

A few moments later, FBI Special Agent Kip Killian strode into the room, closely followed by two other agents, Trigstad and Carter. They all wore crisp black suits and dark sunglasses. When they took off their sunglasses, they were unsure what they were looking at. It certainly didn't look like an FBI facility.

"Director Killian," Ben said, trying not to sound flustered. "Congratulations on becoming the new task force director. That's . . . neat."

Kip Killian wanted this meeting to be over

with as quickly as possible. "Let's save the chitchat," he said curtly. "Time is money."

Ben was nervous. This wasn't going well already. He took a deep breath and began the speech he had been practicing ever since he found out there was going to be a review from the bureau.

"Not many people know that Animal Intelligence Training dates back to the Civil War," Ben offered, trying to sound very academic. "In World War II, dolphins were trained to go underneath German warships to plant mines and explosives. I mean this is a science with no real boundaries," he stated, flashing a smile.

Despite his enthusiasm, the visiting agents didn't seem particularly interested. Killian looked down at a table and noticed an experiment in which Ben was training cockroaches to carry tiny nanocameras into surveillance zones.

"Dr. Kendall," he said as he bent over to

examine the bugs. "Do you mean to tell me Homeland Security is financing a roach motel?"

"It's not just roaches!" Ben replied enthusiastically. He pointed to where Juarez was exercising on an elliptical trainer.

Killian was not impressed. "This is a rodent!" he said.

Juarez stopped suddenly, bringing her exercise machine to a halt. She glared at the special agent.

"Don't say that, sir," Ben warned. "They get highly offended. You know their DNA is 98.7 percent identical to humans, right?"

Killian didn't know, and more importantly, didn't care. Ben continued on their minitour, guiding the agents away from the still angry Juarez.

"Their brains have close to a billion neurons and a trillion synapses," he continued. "That's a thousand times stronger than any supercomputer. It gives them exceptional eye-hand reflexes."

He motioned to Darwin zipping through traffic on a simulated street in a small virtual-reality driving module. Ben thought this was impressive.

Killian did not.

"It's a video game," he scoffed.

Much to Ben's dismay, Killian's mood was getting worse with each demonstration. Still, Ben tried to stay upbeat. "You're probably wondering, 'how does he communicate with them'?"

Kip rolled his eyes. "Oh, it's killing me."

Ben motioned to a microscope on the table. Killian looked through it and saw a tiny electronic device.

"It's a frequency encoder," Ben explained. "It converts sonic information from certain animals into an acoustic syntax discernible by the human ear."

"You're Dr. Doolittle," one of the other agents pointed out, laughing. "You talk to animals."

"Actually," Ben answered, "talking to animals is the easy part. Getting them to talk back is the hard part."

He turned toward the G-Force. "Darwin! Juarez! Blaster!"

The three guinea pigs stopped what they were doing and scurried across various table-tops to Ben's workstation.

"Are we sure these guys are field agents?" Juarez whispered to Darwin. "They look like bank clerks."

Darwin shook his head disapprovingly. "They'll let anything with two legs into the agency these days." Then he clipped on one of the transmitters. "Testing, testing," he said into the microphone. "Hey, how you doing?"

Killian and the others stared at the guinea pig in total disbelief.

"That's . . . impossible," Killian stuttered.

"You think that's something," Ben said with a smile. "Check out Agent Speckles. He's been decrypting the file all night."

"Who's Speckles?" Killian asked.

"He's our mole, star-nosed breed," Ben answered as he pointed to Speckles, who was furiously typing away on his Braille computer trying to decrypt the Clusterstorm files.

"Blind as a bat, IQ off the charts. He's lucky I found him," continued Ben. "His family was exterminated at that executive golf course down by Greenwood."

A beep interrupted Ben. "We're ready," Speckles called out from his computer.

Ben nodded confidently and turned to the agents. This was the moment he'd been waiting for.

"Last night, the G-Force were able to get intelligence regarding Project Clusterstorm."

Killian's eyes narrowed dangerously. "You ran a mission without my authorization?" he asked, his tone angry.

"Yeah," Ben said, trying to act like it was no big deal. "We went to Saber's mansion. . . ."

"Wait a second, Kendall," Killian barked,

his anger turning to rage. "You broke into Leonard Saber's house?!"

Juarez jumped in to help. "We accomplished in one night what you guys couldn't do in two years."

Blaster nodded and added, "And without a warrant." He gulped. "Oops."

"We knew we were up for review," Ben tried to explain. "And we wanted to show you what we could do."

Killian was furious. But he was also a tiny bit interested. They were right. The Saber case had frustrated Killian for two years. Was there really a chance these animals had uncovered something?

"All right," he said, crossing his arms. "What'd you get?"

Taking his cue, Speckles quickly typed on his keyboard, and a diagram started to form on the screen. Everyone looked on with anticipation. But when an image finally appeared, they had no idea what they were looking at.

"What is it?" Blaster asked.

Juarez scrunched her nose as she examined it. "A cappuccino machine?"

Actually, it was a Saberling coffeemaker. And, it certainly wasn't anything that proved Saber was guilty.

"Show them the other file," Darwin said desperately.

Speckles shook his head. "This is all we have. I'm sorry, Darwin."

"I saw that file," Darwin argued. "Ben, give us more time."

There was no more time. Killian had seen enough. "Kendall," he barked at Ben. "Outside. Now."

Ben hung his head and followed Killian and the agents out of the room. Mooch trailed close behind so that the others could watch the conversation on the video feed from his nanocamera.

"Kendall, this entire lab is an embarrassment," Killian snarled. "I'm shutting you and them down."

"Please don't do this," Ben pleaded.

Killian just shook his head. "You compromised a two-year undercover FBI operation. I'm not going to take the heat for this. I'm not going down in Washington as the crazy gopher guy!"

Killian motioned to a pair of black SUVs and out stepped a team of agents.

"Dr. Kendall is coming with me," he told them. Then he motioned toward the building. "Cage anything that moves."

"Cage?" Speckles said with a gulp.

The team nervously looked toward the screen as Killian issued his final order. "This building is Status Six!"

"Status Six?" Juarez said. "What's that?"

Marcie shook her head, her face pale. "It's total closure and quarantine of the department."

On Mooch's monitor they could see the agents approaching.

"Guys," Juarez shouted. "We got company!"

They had to get out—now. Luckily, they always had an exit plan. The escape route from the headquarters took advantage of the system of tubes that Acme Extermination had installed decades earlier.

Originally, the tubes were designed to send capsules carrying bills and other documents from the accounting department to the mail room. Now the G-Force planned on using them to sneak past the FBI agents.

One by one, Marcie loaded the animals into capsules and shot them through the tubing. Before she let Speckles go, she removed his glasses. They would be a dead giveaway if the G-Force were to get caught.

"Yeeeee-hawwwww," Blaster shouted. It was like being on a roller-coaster.

"Not good!!!!" screamed a totally terrified Speckles.

The last one to go was Darwin. Right before Marcie shut the capsule, he turned to her. "Tell Ben that Clusterstorm is somewhere on that PDA. And tell him this isn't over!"

Marcie smiled, and Darwin took off his

voice modulator. He would need to blend in and hide, and he wouldn't be able to do that if people could hear him talk.

Before Darwin's tube could launch, a group of agents burst through the door. Marcie tried to stall them so Darwin could escape, but his tube was malfunctioning!

At the last minute, he was able to get the tube to work, and he zoomed away.

His capsule shot through the tubes, zipping around bends and turns until it rocketed out onto a pile of other capsules. A little dizzy from the trip, Darwin staggered out of his capsule and walked over to where the rest of the G-Force was gathering. He turned to Juarez for a full report.

"What's the situation?" he asked.

"They got the whole lab surrounded," she answered, nodding in the direction of Trigstad and Carter.

Just then, they spied the delivery van from the pet store that routinely supplied the lab with food and supplies. The delivery man, Terrell, had already opened the door to unload when the FBI agents pulled him aside.

"We can hide in here," Darwin said, motioning to a pet carrier in the back of the van.

"Not in the cage," Speckles said, his voice full of fear.

There was no time to think about it. The others quickly scurried into the carrier. But Speckles fought it hard. One by one they went in until the mole was the only one left. He even held on to the edge of the door as Darwin tried to pull him in.

"I don't do cages," he said, straining to hold on.

"Speckles," Darwin pleaded, "let go!"

After a few more moments of struggling, Speckles lost his grip and plopped in with the others. As he did, the cage door slammed shut.

They all shared a nervous look.

"Great," Juarez said. "Now we're locked in."

A moment later, the truck's engine turned

on, and the G-Force were on the go.

As the G-Force agents were riding toward freedom, Special Agent Kip Killian was driving Ben back to FBI headquarters. Ben looked on nervously while Killian spoke on the phone with Trigstad back at the warehouse.

"We're locking the building down, sir," the agent said over the phone. "But the animals have all bolted."

"Trigstad, if those animals bolted, then I've got a problem," Killian responded. "I want them all back. Dead or alive. Zero exposure. Three guinea pigs and a mole, got it?"

Ben was helpless in the passenger seat. He had trained the team well, but could they hold off a full-fledged search by the FBI?

Chapter 5

G-Force had successfully slipped past the FBI only to find themselves trapped. And this time, they didn't have an escape route. The only way out of the pet carrier was through the cage door and that was locked tight. Worse, they didn't even know where they were headed.

Their cage bounced around in the back of the delivery van until it came to a halt right in front of Elia's Pet Shop. When the driver unloaded the van, he was surprised to see the

G-Force inside the carrier.

"Where did you guys come from?" Terrell asked. He was almost certain the carrier had been empty when he put it in the back of the van.

He was especially surprised when he saw Speckles. After all, guinea pigs were common pets. But nobody adopted moles.

"I don't remember ordering a mole-rat thingy," he said, scratching his head.

Terrell brought the carrier into the store and turned to the cashier. "Rosalita, I got a question," he said. "Did you order three guinea pigs and a kind of rat-mole thing?"

"Guinea pigs, maybe," she said, thinking. "But a mole as a pet?" She shook her head no. "Just dunk 'em in there with the rest."

The G-Force couldn't believe what was happening. They were being placed on display . . . in a pet store!

Darwin looked around as Terrell carried them to the back of the store. Almost everything in the store could smell fear. They would have to be brave.

But Speckles was struggling. To him, every animal seemed dangerous. "Okay, I see spiders, some snakes, and b-b-b-bunnies!" he said, totally terrified.

Darwin shook his head. "Guys, we need to find a way out of here," he said, when Terrell had placed them, one by one, into their new home.

If Darwin was nervous, he wasn't letting on. In his mind they were still on a mission to help Ben and to save the program. He had to take charge.

The thought of a mission calmed the others. That was what they were trained to do. As they scanned their surroundings, trying to get a grasp of the situation, Blaster noticed a hamster sitting outside his little home.

"Let's ask that guy," Blaster said. "He looks cute and friendly."

Blaster smiled as he approached the hamster.

"Excuse me, my incarcerated little friend. May I ask you a question?"

The hamster turned toward him and glared. "Don't move!" he snapped ferociously, catching them all off guard. "Know your place! Behind this line!"

The hamster motioned to the floor of the cage, but there was no line. The members of G-Force were confused.

"Is he talking to us?" Blaster asked.

"Did someone order a knuckle sandwich," the hamster said, looking around. "Because I'm about to make a delivery."

Darwin tried to defuse the situation. "Take it easy, buddy."

"For your information, it's Bucky!" the hamster explained. "And if you want to stay alive, do *not* cross that line!"

They looked again and still couldn't see a line, but they decided Bucky was not worth fighting. They needed to focus on the mission. So they just smiled and took a few steps back.

All the noise had awakened a rather fat guinea pig who was in the middle of one of his many naps. Slowly, he rose from his pile of shredded paper and groggily walked over to them. He was a total slob, with crinkled hair, crumbs in his fur, and a huge gut. The first thing he did was let out a huge, long fart which terrified the little mice in the cage with him.

"Name's Hurley. Don't pay any attention to him," Hurley said, pointing toward Bucky. "He's one-quarter ferret."

Bucky glared. "I have no ferret in me!" he shot back angrily. "That has never been proven!"

Hurley flashed a smile. "Then why are you marked down?" he asked. He knew Bucky was sensitive to the subject.

"Everyone goes on sale . . . eventually," the hamster replied, trying not to tear up.

"This should come as no surprise," Hurley explained to the others, "but he grew up in the psych ward at UCLA."

Bucky had had enough. He stormed back

into his hamster house and slammed the door shut.

With Bucky out of the picture, Hurley turned toward the G-Force. "Welcome!"

"Where's the bathroom?" Juarez asked. She wasn't in the mood for chitchat.

Hurley thought about it for a moment. "Well, for me, this morning, it was pretty much where you're standing."

This was too much for the team. They had escaped from Saber's mansion and managed to save Speckles from a killer guard dog. They had escaped from the warehouse and eluded highly trained FBI agents. Surely, they could escape from a pet shop and get away from an angry hamster and a sloppy guinea pig.

"Locate escape options," Darwin instructed the others.

"Stand back," Blaster announced. "I'm going to break the glass."

Blaster took a deep breath, ran full speed to the edge of the terrarium, and threw himself against the glass wall. He hit it with a loud and painful thud and hung there, stuck to the glass for a moment, before sliding down into a heap on the floor.

He couldn't move a single muscle. "This might be a good time for a nap," he said, dazed.

Juarez and Speckles shook their heads. Typical Blaster, they thought, before quickly beginning to search for a way out.

Hurley was confused. "You guys don't want to stay in a place where food falls from the sky, and you can poop wherever you like?"

Before Darwin could even answer, Bucky stormed out of his little house again.

"Okay, okay, the truth is my grandmother met a ferret at the San Diego petting zoo," he admitted. "But nothing happened. They simply dated. My papers say 'hamster.' End of story!"

"Please let me pull his tongue out," Blaster said to Darwin.

"Negative," Darwin answered. "Nobody touches the ferret."

"I am NOT a ferret!" Bucky exclaimed before running back into his hamster house.

Darwin walked over to Hurley. "What can you tell me about our captors? Movement patterns, behavior, anything?"

"Captors?" he repeated. "Your attitude is all wrong. This is paradise! We're safe. We get lettuce. I call it the happiest place on earth."

Darwin sighed. This was not helping. He looked up and spied the hatch at the top of the terrarium. "Let's check that lock," he said, pointing at it. "G-Force, delta formation!"

With expert timing and precision, Darwin and Blaster stood upright and locked arms. Juarez ran toward them, got a quick boost from Speckles, jumped into the air, and came to a perfect landing on their shoulders. It was an amazing move that stunned Hurley.

"Are you guys from the circus?"

"I hate the circus!" Bucky yelled from out of nowhere.

Darwin shook his head. "No. We are

specially bred, genetically altered and highly trained secret agents."

Hurley wasn't buying it, but he was amazed by what he saw as Juarez continued climbing up until she was able to grab hold of the latch. She then tried to wriggle it free. After a couple of failed attempts, she let go and dropped back down to the floor of the terrarium.

"It's locked," she informed Darwin.

"We need another way out," he said, his eyes scanning the area for more possible escape routes.

"Only one way out," Hurley informed him. "In the palm of a loving human hand. You gotta get yourself adopted."

Juarez crinkled her nose. "Adopted?"

Just then, there was a buzzing outside the terrarium. Darwin smiled when he realized who it was.

"Mooch! Go find Ben and report our location," he told the fly. "Clusterstorm launches in twenty-nine hours."

"Who's Mooch," Hurley asked, confused.

"The fly," Darwin answered.

Hurley just shook his head. He'd never known a guinea pig that talked to flies and figured it was a sign that Darwin wasn't quite right in the head.

"Oh, man," he said worriedly. "This usually doesn't happen for several days."

Ignoring Hurley, Mooch flew off. He had to zig and zag his way through the pet store as all sorts of frogs and lizards did their best to zap him with their tongues and turn him into lunch. But Ben's training had paid off, and Mooch made it safely to the door before making his way out through the mail slot.

Darwin looked on hopefully. If Mooch could get to Ben, the G-Force just might be rescued.

Chapter 6

Marcie Hollandsworth sat in her small electric car outside the FBI's regional head-quarters. She looked on hopefully as Ben walked down the stairs and opened the passenger door.

"You okay?" she asked as he sat down and buckled his seat belt.

"I'm fine," he answered. "Tell me you got the G-Force out of the lab."

Marcie smiled. "Yeah, they got out safely."

Ben let out a huge sigh of relief.

"What happened in there?" Marcie wanted to know.

"Well, it went pretty okay," he answered. "Then I got to the bit where I could talk to guinea pigs, and that's when I kind of lost them."

Marcie nodded. That was the part she figured they'd have trouble accepting.

"Darwin told me before he left that he was positive he downloaded the right file," she told him.

"Where's the PDA?" Ben asked.

"It's still back at the warehouse," she answered.

"We've gotta go get it."

"They've probably got security crawling all over the place," Marcie reminded him gently.

"It's okay," he said with a sly smile. "I've got an idea."

"But what about the G-Force?"

Ben smiled proudly. "They're highly professional," he assured her. "They're probably halfway back to my house already."

Unfortunately for the G-Force, that wasn't quite true. While Ben and Marcie were trying to figure out how to break into the warehouse, Darwin and the crew were still struggling to break out of the pet shop.

Blaster was carefully balancing himself on top of the exercise wheel, straining with all his might as he pushed up against the bottom of the terrarium's lid.

"Takes a very steady hand," Blaster bragged, trying to convey how much difficulty he was having. "I hope somebody's getting this on tape!"

He pushed with all his might but couldn't make the lid budge one bit. Then he lost his footing, which sent the wheel spinning one way and him flying the other. He slammed into the floor headfirst. "I think I'll take that nap now."

Darwin shook his head. So far, all of their attempts to break out had failed. They'd need another plan. He turned to Hurley.

"So, how do you get adopted?" he asked.

"Simple," Hurley answered. "You act cute. The kid picks you out, takes you home, and bingo, you're a pet. Part of the family, unconditionally loved forever more."

Just the thought of it made Hurley smile, but the smile quickly turned to sadness. "Except that, they never pick me."

Darwin didn't know what to say. He had never been in a situation like this before.

"Look," Hurley went on. "You're a pet or you're expendable inventory. Life only has meaning when some little kid loves you with all his heart."

"That's beautiful. Truly. I can feel a song coming," Darwin said sarcastically. "But we just need a ride out of here because we have business to take care of."

Just then some nearby mice shouted, "Incoming!"

The animals in the cage all looked toward the door and saw two kids enter the store with their grandfather.

Darwin quickly huddled up with the rest of the G-Force. "First we get adopted," he told them. "Then we escape. Meet at Ben's. Now go act cute!"

They nodded and did their best to "act cute" for the kids. Darwin jumped on the exercise wheel and started running. Juarez rubbed her eyes, trying to look sad and defenseless, and Blaster started chasing his own tail.

"Check it out," he called. "I'm chasing my butt. How cute is that?"

"You're wasting your time till they get past the puppies," Hurley said, leaning back and flashing his big belly. "I should have mentioned that ninety percent never make it past the puppies."

"Grandpa!" the little girl shouted with glee. "Look at the puppies!"

Hurley turned to the others. "Told ya."

The G-Force looked disappointed . . . until they heard Grandpa's response.

"Now, Penny," he said. "Remember what

your mom said. We have to make sure you can keep a hamster alive before we start messing around with puppies. Now, where do they keep the hamsters?"

Hurley jumped into action, doing his best to look adoptable. He gave his paws a quick lick and instantly pulled his messy hair into a stylish swirl.

"Game on," he announced. "Look at me. I'm so sweeeeet."

"Why do you keep doing that?" Bucky asked, coming out of his house. "It's pathetic. No one is ever going to adopt a lazy slob like you."

"You're still here, too, pal!" Hurley shot back. "At least I'm not marked down to six ninety-nine."

All of the animals were doing their best to look cute when Penny and her grandfather reached the terrarium.

"Eeewwww," Penny said, turning up her nose and pointing at Speckles. "What's that?"

Her grandfather scrunched his nose before answering, "A hideous crime against nature."

"I'm outta here," Speckles said, his feelings wounded. He burrowed down under the wood chips.

"It's ugly," the little girl said. "I want a hamster!"

"Yes! Yes! I'm out, baby!" Bucky announced. "Finally! The recognition I deserve."

Unfortunately for Bucky, Penny didn't know the difference between a hamster and a guinea pig, and when she picked one out, she pointed to Juarez.

"Her, with the big cheeks!" Penny declared. "I can put bows in her hair!"

Juarez gulped. "What?"

"What's wrong with you?" Bucky pleaded with the girl. "*I'm* the hamster! They're guinea pigs! Adopt me!"

Terrell reached in and pulled out Juarez, who was not excited about the prospect of being a little girl's dress-up doll. To the people's ears, Juarez was just happily squeaking away, but to the animals', she was already trying to lay down the law.

"You try to put a bow on me," Juarez declared, "you're going to lose a finger."

Blaster turned to Darwin. "That little girl has no idea what she's in for," he said, shaking his head.

"I'm gonna put lipstick and nail polish on her," Penny told her grandfather. "And a dress!"

"A dress!" Juarez squeaked. This was too much. "You're going to lose your whole hand!"

"Juarez," Darwin called out before the lid shut over their cage again.

"I know, I know," she assured him. "Escape and get to Ben's house."

Then Terrell put Juarez into a brightly colored cardboard carrying box shaped like a house and handed it to Penny. One down, three to go.

"It's not fair," Hurley wailed. "She just got here. It's my gut, isn't it?" He looked down at his gut and tried to suck it in. It was no use.

The grandfather called out to the boy. "Connor! Show us the one you want."

As the boy walked back through the store, something caught his eye. It was a toy. He picked it up off the shelf and looked at it. According to the directions, it was designed to throw tennis balls for dogs to chase.

"If I got a dog," Connor pointed out, "we could put a ball in here." He held the ball launcher up for his grandfather, who only shook his head.

"Same deal as your sister," Grandpa said.

Connor deflated a bit and walked over to the cage, still carrying the toy. He could tell that no amount of arguing would convince his grandfather to get them a puppy. He looked at the animals in the terrarium and pointed at Hurley.

"Gimme the fat one," he said.

"Hey! I'm not fat! I'm big-boned!" Hurley squeaked.

Terrell reached in and picked up Hurley.

"Even if you forget to feed him once in a while," Terrell joked, "it really wouldn't bother him. He's a little plump as it is."

Normally, all the fat talk would have gotten to Hurley, but now he was much too excited. He was being adopted—finally.

"Oh, mama," Hurley said. "This is it."

Terrell left Hurley with Connor and went to show Grandpa which aisle had the guinea-pig food. Once the adults were out of range, the boy flashed a mischievous smile and slipped Hurley into the ball launcher.

The animals inside the cage looked on in horror. All except for Bucky, who knew exactly what was going to happen and couldn't have been happier.

"I recognize the look on that kid," Bucky said. "And I love it!"

Hurley, meanwhile, remained oblivious.

"I think he's going to throw him in with that snake," Blaster said, pointing to a snake terrarium down the aisle.

"Hey, Hurley," Bucky called out with an evil grin. "What's fat, smelly, and about to be devoured by a snake?"

Hurley thought Bucky was telling him a joke, but he couldn't come up with the punch line. "I give up. What?"

"You!"

Too late. Hurley realized what was going to happen just as the boy flung the ball launcher, sending the guinea pig flying through the air and into a new terrarium. Hurley landed with a thump in the wood chips. He nervously looked up to see Suzie the snake sizing him up for lunch. She was mere inches away.

Hurley let loose with a terrible shriek, and Suzie moved to strike. When she did, however, her head slammed against a glass wall. Hurley breathed a sigh of relief once he realized that he had landed in the terrarium *next* to hers. Those few inches of terrarium wall were all that separated him from the snake.

"You're lucky I'm not in there, snake,"

Hurley taunted her, trying to sound tough. "'Cause it would have been game over for you!"

Just then, Hurley looked around to see what terrarium he had landed in and realized he was in a tank filled with tarantulas. Spiders scared him only slightly less than snakes. He screamed at the top of his lungs.

"So much for survival of the fattest," Bucky said, sneering.

Just then, Connor reached back into the tank and grabbed a suddenly terrified Blaster.

"Blaster," Darwin pleaded. "Do something!"

"What would you suggest I do?" he asked. He was in the hands of a monster kid. He didn't have many options.

All the mice answered in unison. "Poop in his hand!"

Just then, Connor held Blaster upside down in the air. "Grandpa," he called. "Changed my mind!"

"No no, no," Terrell said, coming to Blaster's rescue. "Not upside down."

Terrell put Blaster into another house-shaped carrying case and handed it to Connor. "Hey, where'd the chubby one go?" Terrell asked.

The boy just shrugged and carried Blaster up to the checkout counter. After looking around for a minute, Terrell finally found Hurley in the tarantula tank. He scooped him up and dropped him back in the terrarium where he belonged.

"You can't even die right!" Bucky exclaimed as he went back into his home.

Ignoring the two, Darwin watched as the grandfather paid for the new pets, and the kids carried half of the G-Force out the door. He didn't like the team to be separated, but he believed in them. He was hopeful they could all escape and meet up back at Ben's house.

"All right, Specks," Darwin said, turning toward the mole. "We have to think of a way out of here."

CHAPTER 7

Special Agent Kip Killian was not having a good day. It started off badly with his visit to G-Force headquarters, where he learned that Ben Kendall had spent all that time and money trying to teach guinea pigs how to be spies. Now he'd have to somehow bury all evidence and reports of the G-Force, and make it seem as though they never existed.

His mood only got worse when he received the latest update on Leonard Saber. For months, the bureau had been listening in on all of Saber's phone calls. They knew he was on the verge of something big, but they couldn't figure out what it was. And they still hadn't been able to uncover any information about the mysterious Mr. Yanshu with whom Saber seemed to be plotting.

Killian took the update directly to his boss.

"At zero-nine-twenty, local time, Saber initiated a call to the usual recipient, Mr. Yanshu in Beijing," Killian explained. "A message was left saying the launch was on track for Project Clusterstorm. Since then, nothing."

The Homeland Security director nodded gravely.

"Kip, our tap isn't cutting it," he said, referring to the listening device they had installed on Saber's phone line.

"If you would authorize a search warrant," Killian offered hopefully. "We'd be able to . . ."

"On what grounds?" the director interrupted.

"I can't authorize a search warrant without probable cause, and he knows it. Saber comes from the defense-supply industry. He knows how to cover his tracks. You give me cause, and I can authorize," he continued. "Keep listening."

Killian was frustrated. "We are, sir."

The director turned toward him.

"Listen harder!"

Meanwhile, Darwin couldn't believe it.

Speckles had come up with his own escape plan. But it sounded way too dangerous to Darwin. After all, even though Speckles was technically part of the G-Force, he wasn't a field agent like Darwin. What he was suggesting was beyond his training. But Speckles had insisted. Darwin had no choice.

Now, Speckles was lying completely still on the floor of the terrarium.

It looked like he was dead.

"Let *me* do this, Specks," Darwin whispered. "I'll come back and get you."

"Relax," Speckles responded, trying not to move his lips as he did. "They told me one of the mice died last week and was buried in the backyard. Once I'm in the ground, I can tunnel to freedom and rescue you."

Just then Rosalita saw Speckles's lifeless body. She came over and poked him with a pen a couple of times. Even though it tickled, Speckles did everything he could to keep from giggling. He had a part to play.

"Terrell," Rosalita called out. "It's dead."

Terrell came over, looked in the terrarium, and frowned. "You're right."

"Well, do something!" she told him. "I'm not going to touch it. Get it out of here before it smells up my shop."

Terrell didn't really want to touch a dead mole either. But he had no choice.

"Hey, trash truck!" she told Terrell. He wouldn't have to bury the mole after all. "Just get it out of here right now!"

Without missing a beat, Terrell scooped up

Speckles's body and quickly ran out the back door. Darwin watched helplessly as Terrell tossed Speckles into the back of the garbage truck.

"No, no!" Darwin called out desperately. This was not part of the plan!

Unaware of the devastating turn of events, Ben was busy trying to get into his warehouse. He and Marcie were sitting in her car outside the old Acme Extermination building. Darwin had told Marcie he was confident there were Clusterstorm files on his portable hard drive. Ben was determined to see them.

He pulled a matchbox out of his pocket and opened it to reveal one of the cockroaches from his nanocamera experiments.

"All right, Harry," he said to the cockroach. "You know what to do."

Ben opened the car door and set Harry down on the curb. The cockroach saluted and started scurrying across the ground to the warehouse.

Ben and Marcie watched as Harry quickly

crawled up the wall of the warehouse to the window of the lab. He turned back and gave them a nod before disappearing inside.

Once Harry got into the lab, he scanned the room and identified the location of the portable hard drive, which was still sitting next to Speckles's computer. His problem was that two FBI agents were guarding the room.

Luckily, he had the perfect distraction in mind.

Harry let out a high-pitched whistle, which was heard by all of the cockroaches living inside the walls, floors, and ceilings of the ancient warehouse. On Harry's command, they started crawling out from everywhere.

Within seconds, the guards were surrounded by thousands of roaches. The guards were scared, grossed out, and totally distracted. In fact, they were much too distracted to notice Harry scurrying across the tabletops to the portable hard drive. He skillfully clicked it free from the docking station and lifted it up onto his back. Cockroaches were capable of lifting

Agent Darwin, the leader of the G-Force,
is ready for his first mission.

The G-Force infiltrate Saber's mansion to
obtain information on the top secret Project
Clusterstorm. They make a narrow escape.

Juarez's martial-arts skills and Blaster's muscles make these two a force to be reckoned with!

Marcie is Ben's right-hand woman.

The FBI is hot on the case.

Ben Kendall always looks for new ways to help the G-Force.

Leonard Saber is more than what he seems.

Speckles knows just the right keys
to hit on the laptop, while Mooch
is the eye in the sky.

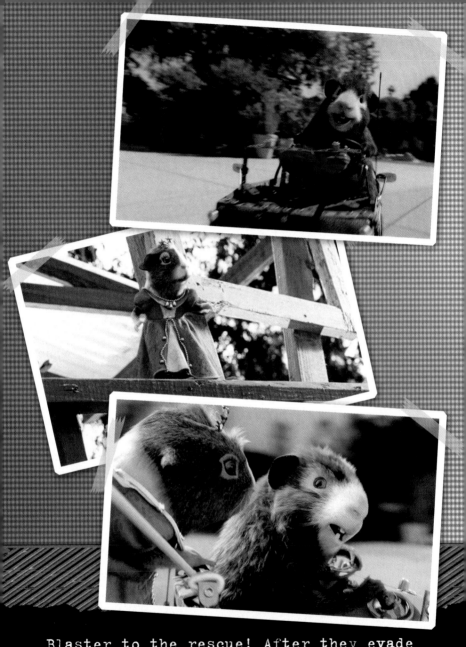

Blaster to the rescue! After they evade capture by a new owner, Blaster and Juarez head back to meet the team.

Time to shine! The G-Force is on their way to stop Yanshu and end Project Clusterstorm. Will they save the day?

The newest members of the G-Force, Bucky and Hurley, are ready to save the world—just don't cross the line with Bucky!

far more than their own body weight.

The giant swarm of roaches kept the guards busy until Harry slipped out the room under the door. When he was safe, he let out another high-pitched whistle. Within seconds, all of the cockroaches had scurried back into the floors and walls, leaving the guards dumbfounded.

Ben watched the front of the warehouse and flashed a huge smile when he saw a tiny portable hard drive moving across the ground toward him.

"Okay, he's got it," Ben called out to Marcie.

He opened the car door, and Harry climbed right up into the car and onto his lap. Marcie gave Ben a smile and then quickly put the car into gear. Soon they were on their way to Ben's house to decrypt the Clusterstorm files.

As they drove, Ben gave Marcie a look out of the corner of his eye. He was lucky to have Marcie. In truth, he normally got along better with animals than he did with people. Marcie was the exception. As a veterinarian, she shared

Ben's love for animals. But more importantly, she believed in him and what he was doing.

Within minutes, they were back at Ben's house. It was old and small, but funky in a good kind of way. It was like a cross between a comic-book store and a laboratory.

Ben took the hard drive back to his desk where he had connected a laptop to a series of computers both old and new. Together they created a sort of supercomputer.

A few minutes after docking the hard drive to his computer, Ben realized that the G-Force had been able to download at least some Clusterstorm files onto the hard drive.

"Darwin was right," Ben said as he looked at the screen. "The file *was* marked Cluster-storm! I've dug down to an echo of the file in the hard drive's memory."

Marcie looked over Ben's shoulder. "Can you open it?"

"I don't know," Ben said as he clicked a button. The diagram of the coffeemaker appeared on the screen. "We've already seen this."

He looked at the image for a moment and noticed the Saberling logo on the diagram. This seemed to be going somewhere. He clicked on the logo, and a bar code appeared on the screen. It was the same one Darwin had seen up in Saber's study.

"What's happening?" Marcie asked.

Ben didn't know. He just shook his head and studied the image. Suddenly, the images on his screen started to melt.

"What's it doing?" Marcie asked worriedly.

"The computer," Ben said. "Unplug the computer."

Marcie reached for the plug, but it was too late. The entire computer came to a crashing stop, and Ben buried his face in the palms of his hands.

"Was that a worm?" she asked.

Ben nodded and held up the hard drive. "This is infected with an extermination virus."

They had no way to get the information they needed.

CHAPTER 8

Night had fallen on Elia's Pet Shop. Inside the cage, Darwin sat, lost in his thoughts. Things had gone so terribly, terribly wrong.

Next to him, Hurley sat, playing with a wood shaving. "You can't blame yourself," he said gently.

Darwin shook his head. "This was my mission . . . and now," he paused, as if the words were too difficult for him, "Speckles is dead."

Hurley looked thoughtful—or as thoughtful

as he was capable of. Then he smiled. He had a way to cheer up his new friend.

Jumping up, he ran over to a pile of clippings. He pulled one out, looked at it for a moment, and let loose a heavenly sigh.

"Cake," he said as he thrust a magazine clipping toward Darwin's hand.

Darwin looked at the picture. It was an old ad for Duncan Hines cake mix. The add featured a picture of a moist, delicious-looking, chocolate cake.

"Cake," Hurley said. "Yummy, frosty, chocolaty cake. This. *This* is why I live."

He took the picture back from Darwin and gave it a big, wet kiss.

Darwin shrugged. He didn't see how this was a big deal, or why it should make him happy. "We eat this every time we celebrate a birthday," he observed.

Hurley couldn't believe his ears. "You've had cake! Let me lick your fingers! Please let me get under your nail! Let me have a taste!"

Hurley grabbed Darwin's paws and tried to get a lick in, while Darwin struggled to keep him away.

"Down boy, down!"

Darwin pulled back, and Hurley fell to the ground. When he did, he was stunned by something on Darwin's leg.

"What is that?" he said, pointing at it.

"You've never seen a birthmark before?" Darwin asked. His birthmark looked exactly like an American eagle.

"I've seen a birthmark before. I have seen *that* birthmark before." Hurley turned around and held his butt up to Darwin. "I have the same one. Look."

"Don't point that thing at me," Darwin said, turning his face away from Hurley's butt. "It might go off."

"Seriously," Hurley demanded. "Look at my butt!"

Darwin held his breath and forced himself to look at Hurley's butt. Much to his surprise, there was a smudged, slightly less cool-looking version of his eagle birthmark.

"I'll admit there's a resemblance," Darwin said reluctantly. "But no. I am a genetically engineered superspy."

"That's what they want you to think!" Hurley replied. "We must have been separated at birth. But fate has brought us back together. My brother! Come here, brother!"

Hurley gave Darwin a big hug, and in return Darwin body-slammed him to the floor.

"Get off me!"

Hurley looked up from his clippings and cuttings. "Note to self. Brother doesn't like hugs."

Darwin stifled a groan. This was not a good day. He was the only member of the G-Force left in the pet store. Speckles was probably crushed. And now he might be related to Hurley. Nothing was going right. Darwin sat there and tried to think of another way out. As he did, he noticed an unusual sound coming from inside Bucky's hamster home. There was some rustling, a little gnawing, and then some unmistakably evil giggling.

"What is he doing?" Darwin wondered as he started walking toward Bucky's hamster house. Hurley followed.

They walked over to Bucky's house and got on opposite sides. Darwin signaled for Hurley to help him lift it up off the floor. He counted to three, and they lifted. When they did, they uncovered Bucky sitting beside a giant stockpile of nuts and berries. Darwin and Hurley shook their heads in disbelief.

For a moment none of them said a thing. Then Bucky flashed a guilty smile and asked, "Can I offer you something? A macadamia nut?"

Hurley never rejected an offer of food—even if he was slightly mad at the hamster for hoarding it. He popped a macadamia nut in his mouth and swallowed it with one huge gulp.

While Hurley was upset, Darwin was

curious. He wondered where the food came from. If no one put the nuts in the terrarium, that meant Bucky had a way to get out and find them.

"This is why I never saw you eat," Hurley said, munching away.

Bucky stood up to him nose to nose. "You drove me to this!" he screamed. "Sneaking out every night to find food and hoarding it so you wouldn't gorge it down." Bucky pointed to Hurley's belly. Then he stamped his foot in anger, and when he did it loosened a trapdoor in the bottom of the terrarium. The door popped open, sending some of his nuts cascading to the floor.

"Uh-oh," Bucky said. His secret was out.

Darwin and Hurley both looked over the edge and down to the floor below.

Now Darwin was furious. "My friend Speckles got thrown in the garbage truck and you said nothing!"

"Take it," Bucky offered, frightened by the

guinea pig's rage. "Whatever you want. It's all yours."

"I don't want any of this," Darwin said, grabbing hold of Bucky and looking him right in the eye. "I want you to show me the way down."

Bucky let out a squeak. "My pleasure," he said. He leaned down through the hole and showed them where a bar was connected to one leg of the table the terrarium sat on. "Of course, the route was designed for someone slightly more svelte," he said, taking a verbal jab at the larger guinea pigs.

"Looks easy," Darwin assured him as he got in position to climb out. "I bet even a ferret could do it."

Hurley looked on. He couldn't believe Darwin was leaving just like that. They had just found each other.

Darwin really didn't know what to make of Hurley, but he did feel bad for him. "Don't give up the dream," he said. "You'll find the family you're looking for."

Nearly moved to tears, Hurley reached over and gave him a huge hug.

Darwin broke himself free from the hug and jumped through the hole. Within seconds he had scurried down the table leg and was on the pet-shop floor.

"So long, brother," Hurley called out as he bent over to watch him go.

As Hurley leaned over the edge, he felt a push from behind. It was Bucky. Before he could catch his balance, Hurley started tipping over and fell right through the trapdoor! He plummeted face-first toward the floor and landed with a hard THUD.

"Good luck with the climb back up," Bucky cackled above him. He knew that an out-of-shape guinea pig like Hurley could never make it back up to the terrarium. "The cage is mine! And it's all true! My grandfather *was* a ferret!"

Hurley looked up and saw Bucky laughing devilishly for a moment before slamming the trapdoor shut. He tried to think of what he should do when he realized that his only hope was Darwin.

Hurrying out the back door of the shop, he saw Darwin trying to use the alignment of the stars to determine his geographic location.

"Go back, Hurley," Darwin said when he saw the big guinea pig lumbering toward him.

"I can't!" Hurley cried.

Darwin sighed. He didn't have time for this.

"I can't," Hurley said again. "I mean, literally. I can't lift myself back up."

Hurley was breathing heavily and trembling as he looked around at the very foreign surroundings. "Truth is, I've never really been out of the pet shop. Can I come with you?"

"No," Darwin stated. "It's a dangerous world out there. Food does not fall from the sky."

The thought made Hurley shiver. "That's all right," he stuttered, trying to sound brave but failing.

Darwin felt bad for him but really couldn't be slowed down. "I'm a secret agent, you're a house pet," he explained. "I'm going it *alone*." Darwin turned and started walking toward Ben's house.

Watching Darwin go, Hurley felt an odd sensation—he felt mad. "You think I can't make it out here!" Hurley called out to him. "You think you're the only one that can survive in the big bad world? Well the truth is, Hurley is out of his cage and it's time to hit the town! Woooohoooo. I'm gonna find me a fat slice of cake and get my freak on."

The more Hurley talked, the more he began to believe in his bravery. Then he heard a cat growl.

"Darwin!" he yelped in terror, racing up to him.

Darwin sighed. He knew it was useless to fight him. "You can come with me," he said, walking on. Then he added over his shoulder, "Until we find you another pet shop."

Hurley nodded, and they started to walk off in the direction of Ben's house.

"Did I mention I'm also scared of the dark?"

Darwin sighed. It was going to be a long night.

At the stroke of midnight, computer chips inside millions of SaberSense electronic products across the globe activated. Instantly, they began communicating with Saberling satellites orbiting the Earth and transmitting information back and forth. Project Clusterstorm was getting warmed up.

From inside his mansion, Leonard Saber was closely monitoring the situation. Sitting at the computer in his study, he tracked the incoming flow of information as he talked via speakerphone with his mysterious partner, Mr. Yanshu.

Despite the fact that Saber was orchestrating an evil plot of global proportions with Yanshu, he had never once laid eyes on his partner. When they talked, it was over a computer. Saber would only see a blank screen and hear a computerized voice.

"So, tell me," Saber said as he looked over a

report. "Why are we spending a large amount of money tracking space junk? Apparently, there are some two million items orbiting Earth: old satellites, booster rockets, bolts, a lost glove, and four million pounds of debris. Remind me, why do we care?"

"Our satellites," Mr. Yanshu replied in his robotic voice. "We have to protect them. Integral aspect of the SaberSense network."

"Of course," Saber replied, nodding. "Now I'm looking at costs here for supermagnetic materials."

"Please don't worry," Yanshu explained. "Everything is going according to plan."

Saber didn't understand all of the costs, but he saw no reason to question the man. "We've got a lot riding on this," he said instead. "I've put my trust in your engineering skills."

"I appreciate that," Yanshu answered.

Saber let out a sigh and shook his head. "It's not easy taking over the world."

CHAPTER 9

Ben was sound asleep in his bed when a fly buzzed across his bedroom and landed right on his nose. At first, he tried to swat it away, but then he stopped.

"Mooch," he said, quickly waking up. "Is that you?"

The fly buzzed a yes and fluttered his wings.

"Oh, man!" Ben said, suddenly excited. "Are the others all right?"

Mooch flew straight up and down to mimic a nodding head.

"You know where they are?" Ben asked.

Once again, Mooch "nodded" yes. Then he flew over to the keyboard of Ben's computer.

"You want me to help you with that?" Ben asked, getting out of bed and taking a seat at the computer.

Mooch landed on the *E* key.

"Mooch, you're a genius," he said as he typed the letter *E*. Mooch flew over to the *L* key and Ben typed that.

"I was so worried about you," Ben said as the fly continued moving from key to key. "I don't like it when my fly is down."

They continued until Mooch had finished his message. He had spelled out the name of the pet shop—Elia's. Ben was ecstatic. Quickly, he grabbed his cell phone and called Marcie. "It's Ben," he said. "I found them! See you in ten minutes."

Calling out a thank you to his fly, Ben

rushed out of his house and hopped onto his bicycle. He didn't have a car, but that wasn't going to stop him. He started pedaling furiously toward Marcie's.

Ben was so excited that he didn't notice the two FBI agents, Trigstad and Carter, sitting in a car down the block. Once Ben turned the corner and was out of sight, the agents started driving straight for his house.

Even if they hadn't been federal agents, they wouldn't have had a hard time breaking in. Ben didn't have any security.

"What a dump," Trigstad said as they looked around. There were piles of papers and experiments strewn everywhere.

"What you got here is your classic dysfunctional male living quarters," Carter replied as he looked for clues that would tell them what Ben was up to. "From time to time you'll find places like this. We just stepped into the mind of madness."

Trigstad sat down at Ben's computer. What he saw made him smile.

"Shut up and come here," he said.

"You found something?"

"We got 'em." Trigstad smiled as he pointed to the computer. There, written right across the screen, was the name ELIA'S.

Carter smiled back, and within seconds the agents were racing out to their car and heading to the pet store. Because Ben was riding to Marcie's on his bike, the agents beat him to Elia's.

Inside the shop, Rosalita was busy. When she heard the door open, she looked up with a smile, ready to greet a new customer. She had no idea what to make of the two who entered the store. With their black suits, dark sunglasses and earpieces, they did not look anything like her normal customers. But a customer was a customer, so she was happy to help.

"*Cómo estás*, gentlemen?" she said, welcoming them with some friendly Spanish.

The two agents ignored the greeting and quickly started scanning the store. "We're looking for some rodents," Carter said.

"For you or your children?" Rosalita asked.

Carter gave her a stern look. "For the government." He handed her police identification sketches of Darwin, Blaster, Juarez, and Speckles.

"What are they, like fugitives or something?" Terrell asked, joining the conversation.

Rosalita laughed, but the agents obviously didn't think this was funny. Trigstad looked at them coolly. "Just answer the question."

Rosalita and Terrell stopped their laughter and quickly got serious. Rosalita told the agents what little she and Terrell knew.

After a quick scan of the store for any possible clues or evidence, Trigstad and Carter left and went to find the family that had adopted Blaster and Juarez.

A few minutes later, Ben and Marcie came into the store. Marcie had been there many times to pick up supplies for the G-Force. Rosalita smiled the moment she saw her.

"*Cómo estás, chica?*" she said, asking her how she was doing.

"Rosie, we're looking for three guinea pigs and a mole," she said.

Rosalita made a funny face and turned to Terrell. "They want three guinea pigs and a mole, too," she said in disbelief.

"Same one as the Feds?" he asked.

Ben was suddenly nervous. "Wait. What Feds?"

"Men in black were here," Terrell told him. "Looking for the same thing. They wanted to know who had bought them."

"Did you tell them?" he asked.

"What do you think?" Terrell answered as if there had even been a choice. "It's the Feds."

Considering the agents' head start, Ben knew that they wouldn't be able to make it to the Goodman house before them.

He was right. The agents were on their way.

Luckily, Blaster was about to live up to his name and blast out before they could even get there.

Connor, the boy who had tried to toss

Hurley in with the snake, had now strapped Blaster into a remote-control monster truck. He was about to run him through an obstacle course of toys and ramps scattered all over his room.

"I'm pretty sure this is animal cruelty," Blaster said as he looked around at all the obstacles. "But I love it!"

This kind of mayhem was right up Blaster's alley. The guinea pig squealed with joy as the car slammed into, raced around, and jumped over the toys in Connor's room.

"Is that all you got?" Blaster shouted when Connor took a break. Just then the boy's mom told him to take out the trash. Connor walked out of the room, leaving Blaster alone.

"What do we have here?" Blaster asked as he looked at the controller Connor had left on the floor.

Suddenly he had an idea. A very good idea.

Blaster slipped out of the truck and took the controller. Then he got back in and smiled as he hit the ON switch and felt the truck tremble beneath him.

"I'm coming for you, Juarez," he shouted as he switched the controller into gear and sent the truck racing across the floor.

Connor had left the back door open when he took out the trash, which gave Blaster the perfect escape route. The monster truck did a power slide across the kitchen's tile floor, and he zoomed right through the door.

"Time for a joy ride," he shouted to himself.

Just then Connor saw him.

"Get out of the road, fool," Blaster shouted.

Connor tried to trap him with the now-empty trash can, but Blaster's virtual-reality training came in handy. He was able to maneuver the car and stay out of Connor's reach.

"Stop it," Connor yelled, chasing after him. "Come back."

"I'll come back when you're a little older," Blaster promised. "And put you in prison."

Safely outside, Blaster raced through the

backyard looking for Juarez. He knew that Penny, the little girl, had brought her back here, but he couldn't see them.

There was a reason. Penny had taken Juarez up to her tree house. She had Juarez all decked out like a dress-up doll and had put her in a dollhouse.

"Juarez?" Blaster called out as he raced around the backyard. "Where are you?"

Juarez heard her partner from up in the tree and kicked into gear—literally. She kicked down the door to the dollhouse and ran to the edge of the tree house.

Quickly, she looked around the backyard until she saw Blaster still being chased by Connor. She shook her head, half impressed that he had gotten out and half worried that he was going to get caught again.

She let out a whistle to catch his attention.

"Juarez!" Blaster shouted joyfully when he saw her. He spun the truck around into a quick U-turn and headed toward the tree house.

With the precision that only a trained secret agent could pull off, Juarez climbed up to the railing of the tree house, jumped off it and onto a trampoline, bounced through the air to the clothesline, and slid along a sheet until she fell perfectly into the passenger seat of the monster truck.

Blaster was thrilled to see Juarez, but he didn't know quite what to make of her appearance. "Why are you dressed like that?" he asked. She looked so . . . girly.

Juarez gave him a mean glare. "One more word and I'll turn you into a small side of bacon."

Keeping his mouth shut, Blaster did some tricky turns to escape from Connor, and he finally managed to zip through an open gate and onto the road.

As they raced away down the street, Juarez started to strip off all the doll clothes and throw them out of the remote-control truck. She did, however, decide to keep one earring. It looked kind of cool.

* * *

While Blaster and Juarez were racing toward Ben in their remote-control monster truck, Darwin and Hurley had found their way to a busy main street. As they tried to avoid the people coming and going into and out of all the stores, Darwin kept looking out for danger.

Hurley, meanwhile, was on the lookout for conversation—and cake. "So," he said to Darwin, "you're telling me you're genetically engineered."

"That's right," Darwin said, keeping it brief.

Hurley looked doubtful. "Face it dude," he said. "You and I are brothers."

The look Darwin shot him was icy. He kept walking.

"What are we doing, anyway?" Hurley asked, panting from trying to keep up.

"Two days ago my team embarked on a mission," Darwin answered. "Today, I'm going to finish it."

Hurley shot Darwin a look.

"Have you always been this . . . intense?" he asked.

Darwin stopped and gave him a serious look. "The fate of the free world rests on my shoulders," he said.

Hurley couldn't help but laugh. "A guinea pig is gonna save the world," he said. "You don't even *have* shoulders! My brother is a loon!"

Just then they reached a bakery. Hurley took a deep breath and pressed his body against the window, suddenly distracted.

"Cake!" Hurley shouted gleefully. "I've heard of places like this! They sell something called layer cake. It's not one cake. It's many! In layers! It's the holy grail of human food!"

Darwin shook his head. "I can't believe you're getting this excited about cake," he said. Then something caught his eye, and *he* got an equal burst of energy.

"Coffeemaker!" Darwin looked through the window of the appliance store at a Saberling

5000 coffeemaker. "That's the same coffeemaker we saw on the Clusterstorm files," he said.

None of this made any sense to Hurley. At least you could eat cake. What could a guinea pig do with a coffeemaker?

"Fifty billion rodents in the world," Hurley said, shaking his head. "And I get stuck with this guy."

Darwin did a quick scan and found a way to sneak into the appliance store. He wanted to get a closer look at the Saberling 5000 coffeemaker.

With Hurley serving as his lookout, Darwin ducked inside and quickly started taking the coffeemaker apart.

"I hope you're keeping track of all those parts," Hurley said nervously.

"Don't watch me! Watch my back!" Darwin cried. "Right now you're my eyes and ears. Just act natural."

Darwin popped open the motherboard and saw the SaberSense microchip that ran the whole thing. The chip had a countdown clock just like the one he had seen on Saber's computer.

"Do you know what this is?" he asked Hurley.

"Yeah," Hurley answered. "I'm pretty sure it's vandalism."

"Military grade, multiple-array transceiver," Darwin said as he examined the chip. "Developed for the military's Unmanned Weapons Program."

Darwin shook his head as he thought of the possible uses of a military chip in a regular household object. "I've gotta get this back to Ben's."

Darwin reached in to pull the chip out of the machine when suddenly, the coffeemaker came to life! Various parts started to twist and turn until the machine resembled a small cannon.

Darwin spun around toward Hurley to warn him. "Duck!" he shouted.

Darwin and Hurley both ducked out of the way just as the coffeemaker started shooting coffee beans like cannonballs. Next, one of the machine's grinder blades whizzed by them and chopped off the ends of Hurley's hair.

They didn't need to stick around to see what happened next. Darwin and Hurley bolted from the store and ran for the street. The coffeemaker-turned-weapon followed them. It had now turned its heating element into a laser and was shooting at them.

"I don't think that thing makes decaf," Hurley said, panicked.

"Come on, move it!" Darwin yelled to Hurley as the machine continued to chase them down the sidewalk past stunned onlookers. But after running a few yards, Darwin stopped and turned to face the coffeemaker.

"Why are we stopping?" Hurley pleaded.

"We're gonna fight it," Darwin explained. "We have to get that chip."

Frantically, Darwin searched around for options to save them. He noticed something in the street. Smiling, he went into action.

"Come on ya tin can," he taunted as he raced out onto the road.

The coffeemaker turned to face him. Watching from a safe distance, Hurley could have sworn that the machine, despite being a machine, actually seemed angry. It charged Darwin.

Darwin held his ground as the coffeemaker got closer and closer. Finally, just as the machine was about to get him, Darwin rolled out of the way—leaving the coffeemaker to be crushed under the tire of an oncoming car.

Darwin took a deep breath as he looked down at the mangled plastic and metal squished into the road. "Don't think the warranty's going to cover that," he said, pleased with himself.

Hurley ran over and threw his arms around Darwin. "I thought I lost ya there. Talk about a killer cappuccino. What is this thing?"

"*This* is Clusterstorm," Darwin said. "Saber's weaponizing his entire line of appliances. We have to get this thing back to Ben's."

CHAPTER 10

A short while later, Darwin and Hurley pushed their way through the doggie door in Ben's house. What they saw inside caused Darwin to stop in his tracks.

Ben and Marcie were sharing a pizza—with Juarez and Blaster! They had escaped!

Marcie had looked happy when the pair had walked in, but then her face clouded over. Something wasn't right. "Where's Speckles?" she asked nervously.

"Speckles . . . didn't make it," Darwin said sadly.

"Gone?" Ben asked, growing pale.

Ben felt a rush of sadness. This shouldn't have happened. He had rescued Speckles from the golf course when the exterminator was getting rid of moles. With Speckles's real family gone, Ben and the G-Force had become his substitute family. Plopping down onto the sofa, Ben held his face in his hands.

"It's my fault," he said, his voice filled with sorrow. "My fault!"

Darwin walked over to him and put a hand on his shoulder. "Ben, there's nothing you could have done—"

Ben stopped him. "I could have told you the truth about who you are," he said sadly.

The team looked at Ben, confused. What was he talking about?

His voice filled with regret, Ben explained that they weren't genetically engineered; they were normal animals with special training. That was it.

111

For a while, the team didn't say anything. They had been living a lie. It felt odd to think about going on as though everything were normal. But then Darwin stood up straighter. He believed in them no matter what. He knew they could do anything. Raising a paw in the air, he cried, "I believe."

The rest of the team echoed him.

Reenergized, they quickly got back to work. Ben picked up all the pieces of the coffeemaker that Darwin and Hurley had dragged with them and spread them across his kitchen table.

"When I tried to disconnect the chip, it came alive and attacked us," Darwin told everyone.

Marcie looked up from the table and right at Darwin. "Came alive?"

Darwin nodded. "The SaberSense microchip caused it to transform. Ben—*SaberSense and Clusterstorm are the same thing!*"

Ben's eyes grew wide as everyone else gasped. That chip was installed in electronic components and appliances all over the world.

"Saber's going to release the world's largest mechanized army, right under everyone's noses."

Juarez looked at the clock ticking down on the chip. "SaberSense launches in thirty minutes!"

What were they going to do? Saber's plan was much too big to be stopped by four guinea pigs, a fly, and a couple of humans. Ben pointed to the portable hard drive that Darwin had used when he downloaded files from Saber's computer.

"I tried to access the Clusterstorm file on your hard drive," he said. "But Saber protected it with some nasty virus that will destroy any computer."

Hurley, who had been busy washing himself, spoke up again. "So why not use that to nix Saber's mainframe."

Ben slowly began to nod. That might just work.

Then Juarez pointed out something the others seemed to be forgetting. Maybe they could pull off a mission like this if they were still at their headquarters. But the FBI had taken all of their stuff. "We don't have our equipment," she pointed out.

Ben flashed a big smile. "Well, that's not *entirely* true."

They all exchanged looks as Ben led them into a workroom. There, he released a secret door and revealed a wall filled with miniature gadgets and devices similar to the ones back at G-Force headquarters.

They all stood and stared for a moment until Blaster broke the silence. "Oh, man, pimp my ride!"

Ben reached up to a shelf and pulled down an unusual contraption that was made up of three plastic balls connected to each other. Inside each ball was a steering wheel, a driver's seat, and levers.

"This is a little prototype I've been working on," Ben said as he showed it to them. "It's called the Rapid Deployment Vehicle or RDV. She'll do sixty-five with the throttle wide open."

Ben looked at Blaster. "You think you can handle it?" he asked.

Blaster's eyes opened wide. "Can I handle it?" he shot back. "It's more like can *it* handle *me*!"

Ben pulled out a tiny set of keys and handed them to Darwin.

"Will you lead this mission?" He would have to infiltrate Saber's mansion, locate the main network core and dock the infected PDA. It wouldn't be easy.

Darwin grabbed the keys right out of Ben's hand. He thought about it for a moment and then looked him in the eye.

"Piece of cake."

"Who's going to take Speckles's place?" Marcie asked as she pointed to a second seat in the back of the center ball.

Hurley let out a big burp.

All eyes turned to him. As unlikely as it seemed to Darwin, Hurley had become part of the G-Force. He would have to take Speckles's spot in the RDV.

Just then, there was a pounding at the door.

"Dr. Kendall, we know you're in there," the voice called out. "Open the door. You have something that belongs to the department."

Agents Carter and Trigstad had arrived.

"Open the door!" Trigstad instructed, knocking again. "Or we'll open it for you!"

Outside, Trigstad and Carter exchanged a look. In a way, they were hoping Ben wouldn't open the door because they wanted to break it down. But just as they went to kick it in, they heard a loud noise. They turned toward the front window just as the RDV went crashing through it.

The vehicle took a couple of bounces across the lawn, and then Darwin threw it into gear. Before Trigstad and Carter knew what was going on, the RDV was racing down the street.

Carter and Trigstad ran to their car and hopped in. "Call for backup," Trigstad said as he gunned the engine. "Tell them that we're in pursuit of three guinea pigs driving mobile spheres."

Carter thought about how silly that might sound over the radio and turned back to his partner. "Actually," he said, "could you make that call?"

Their car tires squealed as they started after the RDV. Blaster looked back over his shoulder and saw that the FBI agents were in hot pursuit.

"Don't these fools know we're on the same team," he complained.

The RDV was moving fast, but Darwin was still trying to get the hang of it as he struggled with the controls. "Juarez," he commanded, "plot us a course to Saber's."

"I'm on it," Juarez replied as she mapped a route to the mansion. Time was running out—they'd have to haul full-speed in order to get there.

Darwin zipped the RDV straight into traffic, dodging the oncoming cars. For Hurley, it was all just too much to handle.

"My stomach doesn't do well with action-adventure," he warned.

"Don't you dare," Darwin pleaded.

There was no stopping it. Hurley was so nervous he let out a huge fart that filled the RDV with gassy fumes.

"Roll down the window," Hurley pleaded.

"These things don't have windows," Blaster replied.

In her sphere, Juarez was gagging. "That's real professional, guys."

Mooch was flying along with one of his nanocameras, sending images of their surroundings to the RDV. On the screen inside the RDV, they could see that two more cars had joined in the chase.

"Okay," Juarez said, "here come the bad guys."

Darwin smiled. "Better have their A game."

The cars swarmed in from different directions, trying to trap the RDV. Just as the cars were about to crush them, Darwin gave the order.

"Unlock it and rock it," he said. "Time to divide and conquer."

Darwin pulled a lever, and the three spheres suddenly split apart and became three separate vehicles, each spinning off in a different direction.

In a flash, the FBI agents all slammed on their brakes to keep from hitting each other. When they did, the spheres disappeared under their cars and raced off.

"Where'd he go?" one agent said. "I lost him."

"This is Unit Two," another said over the radio. "We lost 'em."

In their car, a frustrated Carter and Trigstad looked at each other.

"Face it," Carter said to his partner. "You just got outdriven by a bunch of gophers."

CHAPTER 11

With Project Clusterstorm about to engage, Leonard Saber joined a video conference with his business partners. There were six flat-screen monitors set up in his study. Five of them had live video feeds of the individuals who had helped him get this far. One had no image, just the words, MR. YANSHU—CHINA.

"Members of the Saberling inner sanctum," he addressed the monitors. "My co-conspirators in this endeavor. Our time has finally arrived."

The Clusterstorm countdown clock had reached its final minute and a half. In less than ninety seconds, Saber's plan would begin. "Are we ready to dominate?" he asked with a sinister laugh. "Are we ready to change the world?"

While Saber and his gang were gleefully beginning their world domination, the G-Force was downstairs trying to get past the mansion's state-of-the-art security system.

"Suck in your gut," Darwin pleaded with Hurley as he tried to squeeze his way into a ventilation duct.

"I am," Hurley grunted as he strained to push through the little passageway.

Finally, all of the other members of the team pulled on Hurley until he plopped through the slot and into the duct. After they caught a quick breath, the team started hurrying up the shaft. Time was slipping away.

There was an access shaft ahead. The schematics Speckles had downloaded—what seemed like ages ago—had indicated the computer core was located in the basement. The access shaft would be the quickest way to get there.

Blaster and Juarez jumped into it. But Darwin stopped and turned to Hurley, who was now a full-fledged member of the force.

"This is our exfil," he explained. "It's very important that you stand guard. Whatever you do, *don't* leave this spot."

Hurley nodded. "Got it," he said bravely.

Darwin smiled and jumped into the access shaft. A few moments later, he was in the basement with Blaster and Juarez. Just as he ran up to them, his watch beeped. He looked down and saw that the countdown had reached zero.

Clusterstorm was beginning!

There was no time to waste. They raced forward.

"There's the network core," Darwin said a moment later, pointing to a large computer behind a wall of glass.

They started to run toward the computer core.

As they did, something caught Darwin's eye.

"Hold up!" he shouted.

The three guinea pigs came to a screeching stop just inches from a barely visible wire that stretched across the floor.

"What is it?" Juarez asked.

"It's a trip wire. A booby trap," Darwin explained. "Don't touch it or this place will blow."

The members of the G-Force exchanged smiles. The trip wire was designed to trick a person, not a guinea pig. All they had to do was scrunch down and slide right under it and they would be back on track.

While the G-Force was trying to put a stop to Saber's plan, Saberling electronics and appliances everywhere started to transform and terrorize.

In stores, blenders suddenly whirred to life, their blades spinning wildly. They climbed down from their shelves and formed little robot weapons that were like metal crabs scurrying across the floor and chasing shoppers.

Washing machines and lawn mowers abruptly turned themselves on. They smashed walls and knocked through garage doors. They assembled in suburban streets and roads, forming armies of marching machines.

People everywhere were running from their homes, charging out of their offices, and racing out of stores, all with Saberling products chasing them.

At the Goodman house, where Blaster and Juarez had momentarily lived, the garbage disposal broke out from under the sink and chased Connor and Penny, like a menacing metal spider.

In his FBI office, Special Agent Kip Killian was on the phone, watching in horror as the television filled with reports of worldwide chaos.

Finally, Killian reached his boss on the phone. "It's all Saber," the agent barked, his anger rising. "Is this enough probable cause?"

Before he could get an answer, the Saberling phone he was talking on came to life and sprouted legs. Killian threw the phone to the ground and raced out toward his car. He and his team were going to Saber's mansion . . . with or without authority.

CHAPTER 12

Unaware of the chaos erupting aboveground, Hurley patiently waited at the exfil site. But then a smell caught his attention. A very tasty smell.

"Hmm," he said, sniffing the air. "I better go check the perimeter."

Hurley followed the smell right into the kitchen. What he saw made his eyes grow wide. A slice of layer cake had been placed in a microwave to heat up. It was Hurley's dream come true!

"Come to papa," he said, gasping as he hurried over to the microwave.

The door was open, so all he had to do was step right in. He was so close. Just a few steps and then, just as he went to take a bite, the SaberSense chip inside the microwave came to life. The door slammed shut.

Instantly, the microwave sprouted arms and legs and jumped down to the floor of the kitchen. All Hurley could do was sit inside and hope for the best.

Through the window he could see the other kitchen appliances coming to life. It was just like the coffeemaker.

Then it got worse. The appliances started to come together to form a massive robot creature, with the microwave becoming the monster's head.

"Uh-oh!" Hurley said, realizing he might be in a lot of trouble.

Special Agent Kip Killian and his SWAT team

arrived at Saber's mansion to find it swarming with robot creatures. A vacuum cleaner was flying around the main room, breaking glass and walls. Killian and the SWAT team had to dodge the vacuum and the broken glass as they hurried upstairs to find Saber.

They found him and his assistant Christa trapped in the corner of his study. Saber was using a chair as a defense against a paper shredder that had come to life and was on the attack.

"Saber, what is going on?" Killian demanded as he burst into the room.

"Get us out of here," Saber pleaded, clearly not in control of the situation.

"Take it down!" Killian ordered the team, which started firing on the wild paper shredder.

Meanwhile, down in the basement, the G-Force was trying to plant the virus into Saber's network core when they heard something approaching—fast.

"Determining foodstuff," a mechanical voice said.

Spinning around, they saw a giant appliance monster. At the head of the monster was the microwave. And stuck *inside* the microwave was Hurley.

"It's got Hurley!" Juarez said.

"What's it doing?" asked Blaster.

Darwin looked up and instantly realized what was happening. "It's trying to figure out how long to cook him," he explained.

"Cook me?!" Hurley shouted from within the microwave. He wasn't sure cake was worth getting killed over! "Let me outta here!"

As the team tried to take on the monster, various appliance parts of the creature started attacking the team. A toaster shot at Juarez, who skillfully ducked out of the way.

"Not even close," she taunted as they continued to move closer.

"Hurley, don't be scared," Darwin said, ducking and evading weapons that seemed to come from out of nowhere.

Hurley nodded. "I'm not a chicken!"

It was a bad choice of words. The microwave only heard the word chicken. That was a food it was more than capable of cooking.

"Chicken selected," said the microwave as it started to hum and cook.

Darwin had managed to get up to the machine's head. He pounded on the door, trying to open it.

In a flash, the G-Force came together as a team. Mooch arrived and flew in front of the monster's electronic eye to block its view. Blaster tripped it up with his grappling hook, and Juarez popped open the door to the microwave.

As the creature started to fall, Darwin grabbed hold of an electrical cord and swung into the now-open microwave. Even though his life was in danger, Hurley still hung tight to the layer cake as Darwin pulled him out. This might be his only chance to taste the sweet treat.

Finally, Darwin pulled him out. He dropped

Hurley to the ground, where Juarez was waiting to rush him to safety. Just as Darwin was about to jump to his own safety, the monster stepped back and began to crash.

"It's gonna hit the trip wire," Darwin shouted down to his team.

The G-Force dove for cover as the monster continued to fall. As it crashed to the ground, it tripped the wire, and a giant explosion followed.

When things settled down, Blaster stepped out into the open. The mansion basement was now filled with dust and debris.

"You guys all right?" he asked.

Juarez and Hurley stepped out, brushing the dust off of themselves.

"Can you see Darwin?" Hurley asked.

Juarez pointed. "I see something up there."

She pointed toward the pile of parts that had been the monster. Climbing out from underneath them was a bruised, but very much alive, Darwin.

But they weren't out of trouble yet. The rubble had formed a wall that separated them from each other. Juarez, Blaster, and Hurley were seeing Darwin through the glass that had been the door to the microwave.

"I'm all right," Darwin said, taking stock of the situation. "I'm gonna keep going!"

"Not without us, you aren't," Blaster told him.

"There's no time," Darwin said. "I've got to take down the network core."

The three looked at each other. He was right. They had no choice.

"Huddle up," Darwin instructed them.

Although they were on opposite sides of the glass, they got as close as they could and held up their paws to bump fists.

"We'll be right behind you, Darwin!" Juarez said, her voice catching. "Good luck!"

Darwin smiled and then, turning, he raced toward the still-pulsing network core, leaving the others behind. He followed a series of paths and passageways searching for a spot where he could plug in his hard drive and bring down the computer.

Emerging into a small, dark room filled with computers, Darwin nearly cheered. This was going to work!

Suddenly, an ominous voice called out to him. "Hello, Darwin."

It was Yanshu's voice. But he wasn't talking over a television set. He was in the room. Another computer turned on, illuminating the speaker. Darwin felt his heart nearly stop. He could not believe his eyes.

Mr. Yanshu was—Speckles!

CHAPTER 13

Mooch had managed to find his way through all the debris caused by the explosion and get to the FBI command truck. There Killian, Ben, Marcie, and Saber watched the video feed as Darwin came face to face with Speckles.

"No!" Ben shouted, unable to believe that Speckles was the mastermind.

Saber, who was under arrest and hand-cuffed to a chair, also couldn't believe what he was seeing. "Yanshu was in my basement this whole time?" he asked.

"And he wasn't even a man," Ben said.

In silence, they turned back to the monitors and watched the two former teammates.

"*Yanshu* is the Chinese word for mole," Speckles said with a laugh. "That's how stupid I knew they were. I could put *that* under their noses! SaberSense was just a cover for my real plan. Create an army of robotic appliances and obtain an array of giant electromagnets across the globe that can pull down all the manmade debris orbiting the planet."

"You infected my hard drive!" Darwin cried in disbelief. "And *you* sabotaged our presentation!"

Speckles flashed a devilish smile. "Extermination virus," he said with a laugh. "Nasty stuff."

"We thought you were dead, Specks," Darwin said.

"Oh, don't pretend to care," Speckles shot back accusingly. "Ever googled the word *mole*?" he asked. "Three million entries. Not on how to

135

care for them. No, three million entries on how to *exterminate* them."

"People aren't perfect," Darwin said, trying to soothe the mole. "But you're one of us. You're part of our family."

"My family's dead," he said, referring to his actual family, who had been exterminated at a golf course. "You and Juarez and Blaster. I know you found me disgusting."

"No, we didn't," Darwin pleaded.

Speckles didn't believe him. "It's time for me to go. There are no back doors, no passwords for the program. It's a killing machine."

Speckles let loose a sinister laugh and strapped himself into his chair. Once he was secure, a giant rumble shook the entire mansion as the building and all of its appliances started to assemble into a giant monster, with Speckles at the top controlling it all.

A huge television screen formed the monster's head, and as it rose out of the ground everyone could see Speckles's face.

Also on the monitor, the others could see satellites and other space junk falling out of orbit and being pulled toward Earth by giant magnets. The space junk was slamming into the Earth's surface and forcing people to run for cover.

"You humans stole my home!" he called out. "Now I will steal yours! I will drive you all underground! Into bomb shelters, caves, and the subway. Into the dark!"

He began once again to laugh maniacally. Everything was going according to plan.

But it wasn't.

Darwin had the hard drive with the virus. When the beast had begun to lift off the ground, Darwin had grabbed on to a dangling cable and held on for dear life. Now he began climbing up until he was eye to eye with Speckles. Behind him, the other members of his team held on, too.

"Darwin," Speckles hissed when he saw the guinea pig. "I don't suppose you're here to congratulate me." He hit a button in his command module, and blender blades shot out toward Darwin. As Darwin moved to get out of the way, he accidentally dropped his portable hard drive.

He watched as it hurtled toward the ground far below. All seemed lost. But then he noticed someone standing on a platform lower down on the beast.

"Hurley!" Darwin called out. "The hard drive!"

Hurley looked up and saw the drive just in time. He looked down at the piece of cake still clutched in his hand and sighed. "I *will* find you," he vowed. Then he dropped the cake and lunged for the computer drive, making a great catch.

Darwin let out a joyful shout. "That, brother, is why I got you out of the cage!"

Hurley couldn't believe his ears. "He called me brother!" he said proudly. "Here, catch this, bro!"

Hurley threw the drive as well as any NFL quarterback could have. It arched beautifully through the air and right toward Darwin's hand.

Unfortunately, Speckles saw it flying through the air, too, and at the last moment, he made the monster lurch forward. Suddenly the device was out of reach. Darwin stretched as far as possible but just couldn't catch the computer drive. It disappeared down into the body of the beast. And worse still, Hurley was thrown off the beast. As Darwin watched in horror, his new teammate fell.

"G-Force was never a team." Speckles laughed. "I was your brains, your eyes, your ears. Any last words?"

Darwin slumped. It seemed this was really the end. But then he heard faint buzzing. He looked down and could not believe his eyes. Coming right to him, straining with all his might, was Mooch! And the little fly was actually carrying the hard drive. It took every ounce of strength Mooch had, but he managed to fly all the way up to Darwin.

"Mooch, no!" Speckles yelled.

It was too late. Mooch dropped the drive into Darwin's paw. With lightning-quick speed, Darwin plugged it into the computer's network core. Instantly, the virus went to work short-circuiting the appliances.

"What's going on?" Speckles pleaded as he desperately tried to regain control of his monster.

"Extermination virus," Darwin said. "Nasty stuff."

The monster started teetering back and forth, about to collapse. Despite everything that had happened, Darwin still reached into the control room to rescue Speckles.

"Come with me!" he said, straining to grab the mole's hand.

"No," Speckles responded. "You spoiled everything."

Finally, the entire robotic creature came

crashing down on top of itself. Darwin jumped off into the air and pulled the ripcord on his parasail. He sailed down to safety. When the dust settled, there was a huge mountain of mangled parts and pieces where Saber's mansion once stood.

Darwin made his way over to Blaster and Juarez.

"Where's Hurley?" he asked.

Juarez shook her head. "I don't see him."

"Everybody spread out," Darwin said anxiously. "We gotta find him."

"C'mon, big fella," Blaster called out. "You gotta be in here somewhere."

Ben and Marcie rushed over to them.

"You guys made it!" Ben cheered.

"We lost Hurley," Juarez said. "Help us find him."

Ben and Marcie joined the search and started to dig through the rubble.

"Talk to me, man," Darwin called out. "Where are you?"

Ben shook his head. "Darwin, this isn't looking good. I don't know what to say."

Tears filled Darwin's eyes. "All he wanted was some soft bedding and a friend," he cried. "I couldn't even be that for him."

Suddenly, a voice called out from the top of the rubble. Everyone turned to see . . . Hurley.

"Have you guys seen a small slice of layer cake?" he said with a laugh.

The G-Force cheered, and everyone raced up to Hurley.

"Welcome home, brother!" Darwin said as he wrapped him up in a giant hug.

Juarez, Blaster, Darwin, Mooch, and Hurley all exchanged looks. There was no way the FBI could close them down now. This mission was just the beginning. They would now officially be the G-Force.

And they couldn't wait for their next mission.